GREAT ILLUSTRATED CLASSICS

THE RED BADGE OF COURAGE

Stephen Crane

adapted by
Malvina G. Vogel

Illustrations by
E.R.Cruz

BARONET BOOKS, New York, New York

GREAT ILLUSTRATED CLASSICS

edited by
Joshua Hanft

BARONET BOOKS is a trademark of Playmore Inc., Publishers
and Waldman Publishing Corp., New York, N.Y.

Contents

About the Author

When Stephen Crane was born in 1871, in Newark, New Jersey, he was the last in a big family of fourteen children. His minister father was very strict and wouldn't permit his children any amusements except reading.

Although Stephen enjoyed reading, along with writing and baseball, he rebelled against a formal education and dropped out of college. He then moved to New York City, where some free-lance writing for newspapers kept him from always being broke and hungry.

Then a series of magazine articles on Civil War battles gave him the idea of writing a war novel. While the veterans who wrote these articles described what *happened*, they never described how they *felt*. Stephen Crane would change all that in his novel.

So, although the 21-year-old writer had never been in a war and was writing about one that was fought before he was born, Crane described with uncanny accuracy the fears and sorrows, the cowardice and courage of the soldiers as they fought one of the war's bloodiest battles—Chancellorsville.

Crane couldn't interest book publishers in his story, so he sold it to a newspaper syndicate, and in December, 1894, *The Red Badge of Courage* appeared in serial form in over 700 newspapers. For his 18,000-word story, Crane was paid a half-cent a word, for a total of $90!

The story was greeted with great enthusiasm, especially by many Civil War veterans, who insisted that Crane *had* to have been in the war himself to have described so accurately all that the soldiers felt.

Stephen Crane later *did* report on wars, in Cuba and in Greece. But these assignments left him with his own red badge—malaria and tuberculosis. These diseases led to his death in 1900, at the young age of 28.

During his short life, Crane also published four books of short stories and two books of poetry. But he is best remembered for his classic American novel of the Civil War!

A Union Camp in Virginia

CHAPTER 1

Endless Waiting, Endless Drilling

It was dawn on a spring morning in 1863, and the young Union soldiers of the 304th Regiment were just waking up. Most of the 304th were farm boys from New York State who had enlisted in the army of the North. Now, they were camped in rough log huts and tents on a hillside somewhere in northern Virginia.

From their position, they could see the wooded hills opposite them. Rising above the distant trees were scattered puffs of smoke, the remains of the Confederate campfires that had been burning throughout the night.

For months, the raw troops of the 304th had been at this camp. They had seen no fighting and had only heard reports of great battles between the Union and Confederate armies in this Civil War.

By now, the men were disappointed, frustrated, and bored. They had spent the war drilling endlessly on any open field their lieutenant could find and waiting endlessly for orders to go into battle.

Stretching and yawning as they came out of their tent, Henry Fleming and Tom Wilson, two close friends, headed for the campfire. The regiment's cook was pouring hot coffee into tin cups for the soldiers gathered around him. In between pouring, he was stirring the men's breakfast in a big black pot that was suspended over the fire.

Once breakfast was over, the men scattered about the camp, each looking for ways to keep busy and make the waiting less boring.

Two Close Friends Wake Up.

"I think I'll clean my rifle," said Tom, "even though I did it two days ago. Ain't nothin' much else t' do."

"I guess I'll write t' my ma," said Henry. "She worries if she don't hear from me regular, 'specially with pa dead. I know it's hard runnin' the farm without me t' help."

Before the two started off, they heard shouts from the path that led to a small creek below the camp. Running up the path was Jim Conklin, another of the farm boys in their regiment. Jim was waving a wet shirt high above his head to attract attention.

"Hey, Jim," called Henry, "what you doin' all that shoutin' for?"

"I got news!" hollered Jim, trying to catch his breath as a crowd of soldiers surrounded him. "Listen here! I was just down at the creek washin' my shirt and one a' them cavalry fellers was there waterin' his horse. His brother works at division headquarters, an' he told 'im our regiment's goin' up river t'morrow

"I Got News!"

an' comin' 'round over th' hill behind th' rebels."

"That's a lie!" shouted a corporal. "Yeh don't know what yer talkin' about!"

"Yeah," added Tom Wilson, "I don't believe this army's *ever* goin' t' move. Why, we got ready t' move eight times these last two weeks an' we ain't moved one single step."

The men began arguing among themselves, some believing Jim and others accusing him of making up the story to feel important.

Henry listened to these arguments, first with some doubt, then with eagerness. "So, at last I'm goin' to fight," he whispered to himself. His eyes glowed as he remembered how from the time he was old enough to read, he had pictured himself a hero in every battle throughout history, in every battle in every corner of the world.

So, when this war had come, it was important to Henry to be part of it. His mother had called him a fool and discouraged him. But

Henry's Childhood Dreams of Battle

Henry was determined and had enlisted in a company that was forming in their town.

When he walked into the barn in his shiny blue uniform, his mother went right on milking their cow, though tears ran down her wrinkled cheeks and her thin body began to quiver as she spoke to him.

"Yeh take care of yerself, son. Yeh do what they tell yeh an' don't yeh git in the company of wild fellers who drink an' swear. Remember that yer pa taught yeh not t' think a' anythin' 'cept what's right."

Before leaving to join his regiment, Henry had stopped at his school to say good-bye to his friends. The young people had crowded around him, admiring his blue uniform with its shiny brass buttons and praising him for his bravery. Even the girls looked at him adoringly, and Henry had beamed with pride.

On the march from New York to Washington, the recruits were welcomed at each town. People prepared feasts, young girls smiled

"Yeh Take Care of Yerself, Son."

and flirted with them, and old men complimented them on their bravery. Henry felt like a hero even before his first battle.

But then had come months and months of boredom at this campsite in northern Virginia, where the recruits had done nothing but drill, or try to keep warm, or sit and twiddle their thumbs.

The only enemy Henry had seen or heard was a lone guard on duty on the southern side of a nearby river when Henry was on patrol on the northern side.

"Yankee boy," the ragged guard had called to him, "y'all seem like a right good young feller, a little dumb mebbe for fightin', but right good."

Henry couldn't help but chuckle, liking the man instantly and regretting for the moment that this friendly man was his enemy.

Now, Henry lay on his bunk, excited at the thought that his regiment was finally about to go into battle. But suddenly, he began to

A Friendly Confederate Guard

have some doubts. "Will I be brave enough to stay and fight, or will I be a coward and run away from the battle?" he asked himself.

Henry jumped up from his bunk and began to pace the floor. "Good Gawd, what's the matter with me?" he cried out loud in a panic.

Just then, his two close friends, Jim Conklin and Tom Wilson, entered the tent. They were still arguing over the news Jim had brought back from the creek.

Henry nervously turned to Jim, whom he had known and trusted since childhood. "Are you sure there's goin' to be a battle?"

"Of course!" Jim answered confidently. "Jest wait 'til t'morrow. Yeh'll see one 'a th' biggest battles ever was."

"A thunderin' lie!" grumbled Tom from a corner of the tent.

Henry ignored Tom's grumbling and asked Jim, "How do you think our regiment'll do?"

"Well, I guess we'll fight all right once the battle begins, though lots a' veterans been

Still Arguing Over Jim's News

pokin' fun at us cause we're new."

"Think any of our boys'll run away?" continued Henry.

"A few, mebbe, but that happens in ev'ry regiment th' first time boys're under fire. An' mebbe th' whole regiment'll run if th' fightin's tough at th' beginnin'. But then agin, they might jest stay an' fight real good once they git shootin'."

"And what about you, Jim?" Henry asked with a nervous giggle, as if he meant his question as a joke.

But Jim was serious in his answer. "I s'pose if th' fightin's real hot an' a whole lot a' boys start t' run, I guess I'd run too. But if everybody's a-standin' an' a-fightin', I'd stand an' fight too."

Henry was grateful for his friend's words. They seemed to reassure him that he was not alone in his doubts and fears. "Thanks, Jim," he said softly. "Thanks a heap."

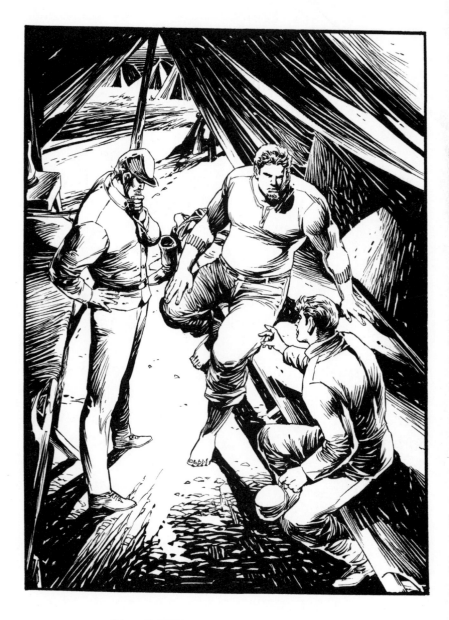

"And What About You, Jim?"

The Regiment Makes Fun of Jim.

CHAPTER 2

Rumor or Fact?

When the following morning proved Jim's story to be only a rumor, the entire regiment made fun of him, even those who had believed him the day before. Henry, however, took no part in this teasing, for he was still troubled by his own secret doubts.

"Will I be brave when I go into battle or will I be a coward?" he asked himself. "If only I could find another soldier who has these same doubts!"

But whenever he tried to start a conversation with any of the men, he had no luck. Each man was absolutely certain he'd be a hero in battle though sometimes Henry believed they were as frightened as he was.

"Should I admit my doubts to them?" he asked himself, then decided, "No! They'd only ridicule me just as they're ridiculin' Jim. I guess the only way I'll ever know the answer is when I actually get into battle."

Days went by, and one morning when the regiment had formed ranks just before dawn, the colonel came riding up on his horse. "At rest!" he ordered.

The regiment stood at rest for what seemed like hours, their eyes fixed on the colonel, who calmly stroked his mustache as he looked across the river at the enemy campfires.

After a while, a messenger came riding up along the road and reined his horse beside the colonel. They had a short conversation, then the colonel called out, "Let's move!"

Cannons creaked and rumbled behind the troops as the men stumbled along through the

The Colonel Waits For News.

woods. They finally reached a road, where other regiments joined in the march. By the time the sun had risen in the sky, the men were certain now that they were finally on their way into battle. And they laughed and sang as they marched.

At one point, the road took them past a farmhouse, where a horse was tied up out front. "Looks like a real fine animal t' carry my knapsack," said a rather sloppy soldier as he left his column and headed toward the horse.

Just as he was about to untie the animal, a young woman rushed out the door and seized the horse's mane. "Leave my horse alone, you thief!" she cried, and she began beating at the soldier with her fists.

This amused the men in the regiment, and they stopped their march and gathered around the two people.

"Hit 'im with a stick!" one soldier shouted, encouraging the woman.

"Leave My Horse Alone, You Thief!"

"Pull that soldier boy by *his* mane too!" shouted another.

The soldier had to let go of the horse to protect himself from the woman's blows. He finally gave up and hurried back to the jeers of his regiment.

"Some hero! Ha!"

"Try goin' after a skunk nex' time!"

"Mebbe *she'd* fight better in th' regiment than yeh!"

Still in good spirits, the troops continued their march until nightfall, when they broke up into individual regiments. They set up tents in the fields and lit campfires.

Henry lay down in the grass a distance from the other men in his regiment. He wanted to be by himself.

After a while, Tom Wilson walked over to him. "What yeh doin' way over here, Henry?"

"Oh, thinkin'."

Tom sat down and slowly lit his pipe. He took a long drawl, then smiled gleefully. "We

Jeered by the Regiment

got 'em now, Henry! We're goin' t' lick 'em good!" Then Tom turned serious. "Actu'lly, *they've* been lickin' *us* in ev'ry battle 'til now. But this time, I feel it in my bones—we'll lick 'em! We'll lick 'em good!"

"I thought you were objectin' to all this marchin'," Henry said coldly.

"I don't mind th' marchin' long as there's fightin' at th' end a' it. What I hate is gettin' moved here an' moved there, with nothin' bein' gained 'cept sore feet an' short rations."

"And how do you know *you* won't turn and run when the fightin' starts?" Henry asked.

"Run?" cried Tom, jumping up. "Course not! I'll do my share a' fightin'. An' besides, who do yeh think yeh are t' question me, th' gen'ral or somethin'?" With that, he strode angrily away.

"Well, you needn't get so mad about it!" Henry called after him. Then he stood up and slowly made his way back to his tent.

"I'll Do My Share a' Fightin'."

Crossing a River on Pontoon Bridges

CHAPTER 3

A First Battle

The march continued the following day. By nightfall, the regiments reached a river. They set up two pontoon bridges and crossed over to face a mysterious range of hills.

Henry peered up at the hills as he stood on the river bank. "The rebs must be hidin' in those dark woods, just sittin' and waitin' for us," he told Tom.

But once the weary troops set up camp, they had a peaceful night's sleep.

The next morning, the regiment entered a deep, thick forest. They spent several days marching and camping through it until one gray dawn when Jim kicked Henry awake.

"What in thunder—?" Henry gasped as he jumped to his feet.

"We're movin', Henry. Hurry!"

And before he was completely awake, Henry found himself with the other men in his regiment not marching, but running breathlessly, down a road in the woods.

"What th' devil they in sech a hurry for?" Tom yelled out to his comrades.

But no one had any answers for him. And no one dared stop running. Each man feared that if he stopped, the mob of troops running behind him would surely trample him to death.

By the time the sun appeared in the sky, other regiments were joining them. "It's time," Henry told himself. "The battle is about to begin and I'm about to be tested. Even if I wanted to escape, it's impossible. Troops are surroundin' me on all sides. It's like bein' in a movin' box."

Jim Kicks Henry Awake.

THE RED BADGE OF COURAGE

Henry's head seemed to be fighting what his body was doing. "I didn't want t' be in this war," he argued. "I didn't enlist on my own; the government is takin' me out t' be killed." But he knew this wasn't so!

"Run, Henry, run for your life!" he told himself. And along with his regiment, he slid down the bank of a stream and waded across, with his rifle held high above his head.

As the troops scrambled up the bank on the other side, cannons began to boom. The men climbed up a hill expecting to see a battle scene in the field below. But they found only small lines of their skirmishers. Those soldiers were usually sent out in front of the main army to clear the way for a major attack. The skirmishers were now firing into the trees to rout out any enemy soldiers.

As the regiment began crossing the field, they came upon the body of a Confederate soldier. Most of the men walked around it with hardly a glance. But this was the first corpse

Wading Across a Stream

Henry had ever seen, and he stopped and stared down at it. The man's open eyes gazed up, unseeing, at the sky, and his brownish-yellow beard blew in the wind.

Henry's eyes traveled down to the man's shoes. The soles were worn so thin that one of the soldier's feet stuck out through a large hole. "How sad!" he thought. "This man must've been so poor that he couldn't even afford t' have his shoes fixed!"

All kinds of crazy ideas began to creep into Henry's head as he marched along with his regiment. "Our generals don't know what they're doin'. They're leadin' us into a trap. Soon we're goin' t' be surrounded by those rebs. I'd better warn my comrades that the generals are idiots!"

But as he looked around, Henry saw that his comrades were so fascinated with their advancing march, they would surely laugh at his warning. Dejected, he began to lag behind the other marchers.

The First Corpse Henry Has Ever Seen

Seeing this, the lieutenant came up to him and tapped at his back with his sword. "Move along, soldier!" he ordered. "Get up into your ranks and stop laggin' behind."

Henry hurried to rejoin the line, hating the lieutenant and all of the officers in the company. "Stupid fools!" he muttered under his breath.

A halt was called to allow the skirmishers to advance farther into the woods. During the halt, the troops began to build small hills in front of them, using stones, dirt, sticks, and anything that might stop or deflect a bullet. These hills caused some arguments among the men.

"I'll *stand* t' do my fightin'!" Tom said with a sneer at the men digging trenches.

"Whatever suits yeh," snapped Jim. "But look around at th' veterans down th' line. They're diggin' up holes like dogs buryin' their bones. They must know somethin'."

Not too long afterward, however, the 304th

"I'll *Stand* T' Do My Fightin'!"

was ordered forward and the men had to leave their newly built hills behind. This happened once, then twice more. Finally, when they were ordered to halt and dig in for a third time, Henry's anger exploded.

"What did they march us here for if we're goin' t' change position each time we feel safe? I can't stand this much longer! All we're doin' is wearin' out our legs for nothin'!"

Jim took out his rations and carefully made a sandwich of pork and crackers. After swallowing it easily, he explained, "I guess we have to explore this here country t' keep the rebs from gittin' too close."

"Well, I'd rather do most anythin' than go trampin' 'round the country doin' no good and jest tirin' myself out!" argued Henry.

"So would I," added Tom as he came over to sit with his friends. "It ain't right. If anybody with any sense was a-runnin' this army, it—"

Wearin' Out His Legs for Nothin'!

"Oh, shut up, yeh little fool!" roared Jim. "Yeh ain't had that uniform on for more 'n six months and yeh talk as if—"

"I came here t' fight and not t' walk!" argued Tom. "If I jest wanted t' walk, I could've walked round an' round my barn at home."

Jim threw up his hands in despair and began making himself another sandwich. As he ate, he returned to being his usual calm self.

That afternoon, as the regiment continued their march with no obvious destination, Henry again began to doubt the general's sanity in leading the troops. "The way that man's directin' this battle, I might as well end my troubles and get killed right away. That's better than goin' on this way, not knowin' when those rebs are goin' t' put a bullet in me."

At that moment, rapid firing in the distance sent shock waves through the troops. Flashes of enemy musket and rifle fire

"Shut Up, Yeh Little Fool!"

scattered the skirmishers advancing ahead of them. Then an explosion from a Confederate cannon landed on the regiment in front of the 304th and sent bodies flying.

Henry stared with his eyes and mouth frozen wide open. When he felt a hand on his arm, he swung around in panic. "Oh, Tom, it's you," he gasped in relief.

Then, seeing his friend's pale, terrified face, he asked, "What's happened, Tom? I've never seen you look like this before."

Tom's lips were trembling as he answered, "This is goin' t' be my f-first an' last battle, Henry. Somethin' tells me I w-won't come out of it alive—"

"Stop talkin' such craziness, Tom!"

"No, listen. I w-want yeh t' take these here things t' my folks." With a sob, he handed Henry a thick yellow envelope.

"What the devil—" But before Henry could say another word, Tom waved a weak good-bye and walked away.

"Take These Here Things T' My Folks."

Shot in the Hand

CHAPTER 4

A Wild Retreat

The troops of the 304th moved up to the edge of the grove. They crouched and pointed their guns toward the open field, where another regiment was under fire. Though thick smoke covered everything, they could make out men running and shouting to each other.

Screaming shells were whizzing into the grove, sending branches and leaves down on the heads of the regiment hiding there.

The lieutenant out on the field was shot in the hand. He held it away from his body so the blood wouldn't drip on his uniform. This gave the men of the 304th a chuckle.

When his captain came to his aid and bandaged the wound with his handkerchief, the two officers got into an argument as to exactly how the bandaging should be done.

"Officers, hah!" muttered Henry, more certain than ever that officers were stupid.

He turned away from the officers and back to the troops under fire. Through the smoke and flashes of gunfire, he spotted the regiment's battle flag flying toward him in the grove. Following the flag was a mob of screaming soldiers wildly fleeing the battle.

Officers on horseback rode frantically among the deserting men, cursing and threatening them, striking them with their fists, kicking them with their legs, and beating them with their swords, all in a futile attempt to keep them on the battlefield.

"Go back, you cowards! Go back!"

"Stay and fight! Fight like men!"

A Foolish Argument Over Bandaging

"Pick up that gun and shoot! Shoot!"

But the stampede continued.

The flag bearer was running toward the grove with the rest of his regiment when a bullet hit him. He fell to the ground, taking the flag down with him.

In the grove, the veteran troops on either side of the 304th regiment began to jeer at the fleeing soldiers.

"What th' devil yeh in sech a hurry fer?"

"Yeh run like a herd a' cows!"

"O Gawd! They're as raw as fresh fish!"

Henry looked up and down the line at the raw recruits in his own regiment as they stood in the safety of the trees watching the wild retreat in front of them.

"Why, they're pale an' shakin' with horror just like me," he thought. "We ain't seen them rebs out in the open yet, but I guess when we do, we'll all be ready to run away, just like that regiment out on the field is doin' right now!"

Watching a Wild Retreat

The Rebel Attack Begins.

CHAPTER 5

The Rebels Attack

"Here they come!" called the lieutenant, waving his sword. And his cry was repeated throughout the grove. "Here they come!"

The soldiers opened their cartridge boxes and quickly began loading their rifles.

From out of the smoke-filled field in the distance came a swarm of running, yelling rebel soldiers. At the front, the bright red and blue Confederate flag stood out against the men's dust-covered gray uniforms.

The Union general rode wildly up to the front of his line, shaking his fist and shouting savagely at the colonel, "You've got to hold them back! You've got to!"

The colonel replied, "We'll do our best, sir. I'll give my captain the orders now."

Hearing the officers talking, Tom Wilson mumbled to Henry, "We're in for it now!"

Once the captain received the orders, he began pacing up and down the line behind the men, repeating to each position, "Hold your fire, boys. . . . Don't shoot till I tell you to . . . . Save your fire till they're close up."

Henry's face was dripping with perspiration, which he nervously wiped with his coat sleeve. When the "Fire!" order finally came, he raised his rifle and wildly fired off his first shot. His next ones were better aimed.

All around him, bullets from the rest of the troops joined with his to blaze toward the rebels. As he fired, Henry felt a rage building up in him. A burning roar filled his ears, a blistering sweat rolled down his face, and his eyeballs felt like hot stones.

"Save Your Fire Till They're Close Up."

THE RED BADGE OF COURAGE

He became furious at his rifle because it could only kill one man at a time. He became more furious at himself because he couldn't destroy the entire rebel army with one shot.

Noises of the regiment cheering, praying, snarling, even babbling, surrounded Henry. Mixed with these noises was the clanking and clanging of the steel ramrods, which the men pounded into the hot barrels of their rifles as they loaded each new cartridge.

With the cartridges in place, the soldiers jerked their rifles onto their shoulders and fired. Some fired aimlessly into the smoke; others fired at the blurred, moving forms that were advancing toward them.

The officers were running back and forth, observing the enemy on the other side of the smoke, then shouting out orders and encouragement to their own men.

Henry's regimental lieutenant was gripping the collar of a weeping soldier who had fled screaming when the shooting began. He

Stopping a Fleeing Soldier

was slapping the young man and pushing him back into position to start firing.

Soldiers were dropping like bundles all around Henry. One soldier was holding his head and babbling after being grazed by a shot that sent the blood streaming down his face. Another gripped at the bullet hole in his stomach as he slid down to the ground.

Up the line, a man stood with both arms clinging desperately to a tree. He was crying, "Help me! Someone please help me! My knee's been split open by a bullet!"

After a while, the firing quieted down on the field in front of the 304th. When the smoke finally cleared, Henry saw that the enemy had been driven back and scattered into small groups.

All around him, the battle-weary troops had different reactions to the victory. Some were whooping wildly. Others sat stunned, staring at the bodies scattered on the ground and at their wounded comrades who were

"Someone, Please Help Me!"

trudging wearily toward the rear.

Grimy, exhausted, and dripping wet with perspiration, Henry found it difficult to take a deep breath. He reached down for his canteen and took a long swallow of water. It refreshed him. "It's over at last!" he whispered to himself with a deep sigh and a smile. "And I reckon I've done right well."

He stood up, filled with a new feeling of good will toward his comrades. "Sure is hot, ain't it?" he called to a nearby soldier who was stretched out on the grass.

"You bet!" the man replied. "An' I sure hope we don't have no more fightin' till a week from Monday."

Henry's good will continued as he shook hands with more of his comrades and helped one soldier bandage a wound on his shin.

All of a sudden, cries of amazement broke out along the line. "Here they come again!"

Henry turned quickly toward the field and saw rebel troops pouring out of the distant

Helping a Wounded Comrade

woods with their flag bearer in the lead.

Shells began exploding again in the trees and in the grass as the enemy approached. The men of the 304th moved their exhausted bodies stiffly, and their grimy faces showed just how discouraged they were.

"Why can't those gen'rals send us some re-placements?" complained a corporal.

"We ain't never goin' t' put down this second attack!" argued Jim.

"I didn't come here t' fight th' whole rebel army myself!" snapped Tom angrily.

"This has to be a mistake," mumbled Henry, not believing what was happening. But the sheets of flame and clouds of smoke along the line convinced him there was no mistake.

The muscles in his arms and legs went numb. The nerves in his neck pounded the blood into his head. "If those enemy troops could attack again so soon, they have to be machines, not men!"

Henry lifted his rifle and began to shoot

Panicking over the New Attack!

into the smoke. Each time the smoke cleared, he was able to see the rebels coming closer and closer. "They're like attackin' dragons comin' to gobble me up!"

His comrades saw the same "dragons." Men who had been shooting courageously suddenly threw down their rifles and fled from the battlefield. Over and over, these frightened troops rushed past Henry.

"They're runnin' away!" he gasped. "Runnin' like scared rabbits!" Then he added with horror, *"And they're leavin' me behind! They're leavin' me t' fight the whole rebel army by myself!"*

When that horrifying realization hit him, Henry gave a frightful yell. He jumped up, threw down his rifle, then sped to the rear in great leaps. His hat flew off and his unbuttoned coat flapped in the wind. His canteen swung out behind him, and the lid of his cartridge box bobbed wildly.

He ran like a blind man, falling over rocks,

Fleeing in Horror!

banging into trees, hearing only the footsteps of the men running beside him, behind him, and in front of him.

Officers tried to force the troops back to their positions, but it was no use. The shells screaming over their heads made the men run even faster.

One shell exploded like lightning on the ground directly in front of Henry, sending him flying head first into the dirt. Moments later, he sprang up and fled into the safety of some bushes.

He passed close to a battery of six cannons under attack from the enemy across the field on a hillside. The men seemed to be patting the thick, black barrels of the cannons as they loaded the balls into them and lit the fuses.

"Fools!" gasped Henry. "Idiotic fools! They're so enthusiastic about what they're doin', they don't realize they'll be dead before long!"

Cannons Being Loaded

THE RED BADGE OF COURAGE

When the shooting seemed to be far enough behind him, Henry slowed his pace. It was then that, through some thick bushes, he saw a general and several officers seated on their horses. A young cavalryman was riding toward them, waving excitedly.

Henry crept through the bushes, thinking, "If I'm right quiet here, maybe I'll find out what's happenin' back on the front line. Or maybe I'll tell that general about the fix my regiment's in and how they sure need orders to retreat."

"Good news, General!" cried the rider. "Your plan worked! The line held! The regiments didn't have to retreat!"

"By heavens, they've held 'em!" shouted the general, bouncing excitedly in his saddle. "My boys held the line against those rebels! We'll wallop 'em now! We've got 'em for sure! Let's get over there and congratulate those boys!"

"We'll Wallop 'Em Now!"

Cringing in Shock!

CHAPTER 6

A Horrible Discovery!

"They won after all!" gasped Henry, cringing in the bushes. "Those idiots stayed and won! Those blind, stupid men didn't have the good sense to realize they couldn't possibly hold that line. But they did. . . . Now, what are they goin' t' say when I get back there? Sure as shootin', they're goin' t' torment me an' shame me!"

Once the officers had ridden off, Henry stood up and angrily trudged on, heading into thicker woods where vines and bushes and trees grew close together. There was no path and he had to force his way through, separating vines from bushes and bushes from trees. He hoped that the noises of the branches swinging back into place didn't alert nearby soldiers who might be looking for him.

On he went, deeper and deeper into the woods. The sounds of war and death were now gone. Only the buzzing of insects and the singing of birds reached his ears. Only the sunlight blazing through the trees looked for him. It was a time of total peace for Henry, and he didn't want it to end.

A playful squirrel crossed his path and stopped to stare at him. Henry threw a small pine cone toward the furry creature. Chattering with fear, the squirrel scampered off and climbed to the top of a tree. There, safe on a branch, he stopped and looked down in fright at the blue-coated stranger.

Henry raised his head and smiled. "You have obeyed the laws of Nature. You're

Meeting a Playful Squirrel

smarter than all those boys back in the regiment. You saw you were in danger and you ran, just like I did. You didn't stand there and wait for the pine cone to hit you, just like I didn't wait for those bullets to hit me. Yes, siree, we sure are smarter!"

Henry continued on deeper into the woods. After a while, he reached a place where the tall branches curved into an archway. It reminded him of the archway in a church chapel, with the sunlight streaming in. Some bushes seemed to act as the chapel door. Pushing the bushes aside, Henry entered.

But he immediately froze in his tracks, horrified at the sight that greeted him. There, seated with his back up against a thick tree trunk, was a dead man! Sticking out above his faded blue uniform was a ghostly gray face. Its eyes stared out at Henry, much as the eyes of a dead fish stare out at the fisherman who caught it. The mouth of the corpse hung open.

A Ghastly Sight in a Forest Chapel!

THE RED BADGE OF COURAGE

Henry stopped breathing for a moment, then gave a shriek. Carefully placing his hands behind him, one at a time, he groped for the support of a tree. Then he backed out of the chapel, step by step, never once taking his eyes off the corpse for fear that the thing might jump up and follow him!

Once outside, Henry turned and fled, paying no attention to the vines and bushes and thorns that tore at him. All he could see was that dead gray face! All he could hear were strange voices that he imagined were coming from that dead throat... voices that were shouting out, "Henry Fleming! Coward!"... voices that were accusing, "Henry Fleming! Deserter!"

The peace in Nature was gone!

Backing Away in Terror!

Running Through the Silent Woods

CHAPTER 7

Joining the Wounded Throng

Henry kept running until the sun began to sink in the sky. By then, the voices in his head had slowly faded, and he heard only the rustle of the trees in the silent woods.

Then, suddenly, in the distance, the thunderous roar of cannons and the exploding blasts of rifles broke the silence. Henry stopped running and listened. "It's startin' again," he whispered. "Only now it seems worse than the fightin' I ran away from."

When he started running again, Henry realized that his feet were leading him toward the edge of the woods... *toward* the battle. "Why am I headin' for a war I just ran away from?" he asked himself. And he knew why. "That shootin' means this must be an important battle, and I just got t' see it!"

The louder the battle noises grew, the faster Henry ran. Soon he left the safety of the woods and was heading across a field.

He climbed over a fence that ran along the field. On the far side, he found the ground covered with clothes and guns... and five dead soldiers! "They must've been dead for some time out here in the hot sun," he decided, "judgin' from the looks of their swollen bodies."

A chill suddenly ran through him, and he hurried off, fearful that one of the corpses would rise and chase him away.

By the time night was approaching, Henry saw a road in the distance. As he came close, he saw a stream of blood-stained troops stumbling along, groaning, cursing, and wailing

Corpses on a Battlefield

with each step they took.

One soldier was laughing hysterically as he hobbled along like a school child playing hopscotch . . . but this man was hobbling in a shoe full of blood!

Another soldier was staring blankly ahead as he marched along, playing an imaginary drum and singing his version of a child's song:

> "Sing a song a' vic'try
> A pocketful a' bullets,
> Five an' twenty dead men
> Baked in a . . . pie."

Others soldiers were leaning on their rifles as they walked, their faces twisted in agony.

One man seemed moments away from death as his bloody hands covered a wound in his chest and his teeth bit into his lips.

A wounded officer being carried along by two privates bellowed at the men, "Don't joggle me so, you fools! My leg's not made

Agonized, Wounded Soldiers

of iron!" Then he turned his rage on the limping troops in front of him. "Make room for me or I'll knock you down, you fools!"

Messengers occasionally rode through the crowd, scattering the wounded to the side of the road. Officers galloped through as well, shouting "Clear the way!" when cannons had to break into the throng to be repositioned.

Henry joined the crowd and trudged along beside a tattered, ragged man who was covered from his hair to his shoes with blood, dust, and powder stains. A blood-soaked rag was tied around his head, and another was wrapped around his limp arm, which dangled at his side like a broken tree branch.

Trying to be friendly, the man smiled at Henry. "It was a pretty good fight, wasn't it, young feller?" he said weakly.

"Y-yes," muttered Henry. Then, to avoid further talk of battle, he hurried on ahead.

But that didn't stop the tattered man, and he hobbled along to keep pace with Henry and

"Make Room for Me!"

start the conversation again. "Derned if I ever did see fellers fight so good! They ain't had no fair chance up t' now, but this time they showed 'em. Yes, sir! I tell yeh, they be fighters, they be!"

Henry continued to ignore the tattered man, but the veteran had more war stories to tell. "And once I was talkin' 'cross a wall with a boy from Georgia an' he sez t' me, 'Yer fellers'll all run once they hears our guns.' Well, I din't b'lieve none of it an' I larfed. An' t'day our fellers din't run. No, sir! They stayed an' fought an' fought an' fought."

He put his good arm on Henry's shoulder and asked, "Where yeh hit, young feller?"

Panic took hold of Henry. "Why, I-I—that is—I—" be began nervously. Then he turned quickly and hurried off the road, away from the throng.

The tattered man stood staring after him in astonishment.

"Where Yeh Hit, Young Feller?"

Hiding from the Tattered Soldier

CHAPTER 8

Jim Conklin's Red Badge of Courage

Henry hid behind some trees and waited until the tattered soldier had gone on ahead. Then he returned to the road and joined the throng. But the tattered man's question kept echoing in his ears: *"Where yeh hit, young feller?"*

Now, as he looked around at the wounded soldiers, he envied them. "They've earned their red badge of courage. Every bloody wound they got is a red badge for them."

When any of the men looked back at him, Henry immediately turned away. "They know what I've done and they're ashamed of me. If only I could earn my own red badge of courage!" he wished silently.

When he finally noticed the soldier beside him, his first reaction was: "The man looks like a walkin' ghost!" His eyes were staring into some unknown space straight ahead and never once turned to the side. And his grim, tightly pressed lips seemed to be holding back great pain.

As the man walked stiffly along, his eyes began to move from side to side, as if they were searching for something in the grass. "It's almost as if he's searchin' for a place t' die!" Henry whispered to himself.

As if he heard the whispered words, the man slowly turned his head toward Henry.

The shock of seeing the pale, waxlike face made Henry gasp! "My Gawd! It's you, Jim! Jim Conklin!" he screamed.

The soldier smiled weakly and whispered, "Hello, Henry." And he held out his blood-

Shocked at Recognizing Jim Conklin!

covered hand. "Where yeh been? I was worryin' mebbe yeh got kilt. There's sure been thunder t' pay t'day. Where yeh been?"

Henry's legs weakened, and he moaned over and over, "Oh, Jim—oh, Jim—oh, Jim—"

"Yeh know, Henry, I got shot," Jim mumbled in a confused way. "Don't 'xactly know how it happen'd, but by jiminey, I got shot."

Henry reached out his arms to help his old friend, but Jim insisted on walking alone.

They walked beside each other for a while. Then Jim suddenly stopped and looked around in terror. He clutched Henry's arm, leaned close, and whispered, "I'm 'fraid, Henry. I'm 'fraid I'll fall down an' them cannons an' artillery wagons'll run over me."

Henry cried out hysterically, "I won't let that happen, Jim. I'll take care of you!"

"Are yeh sure, Henry? Really sure?" Jim's eyes rolled in terror as he clung to Henry's arm like a child clings to his mother. "I was a good friend t' yeh. An' it ain't much

"I'm 'Fraid, Henry."

t' ask, is it? Jest pull me out a' th' road if'n I fall."

Henry's sobs made it impossible for him to answer. All he could do was nod and grip his friend's arm a little tighter.

But Jim pulled away to walk ahead. It was as if he had forgotten his fear of falling. "Leave me be," he said, and Henry did as his friend asked.

After a while, Henry felt a hand gently tap him on the shoulder. It was the tattered soldier he had run away from earlier.

The man began talking softly. "Yeh'd best take yer friend out a' th' road, young feller. There's a load a' cannons comin' along right fast, and yer friend'll git runned over. He ain't got more 'n five minutes t' live anyhow, yeh kin see that. Don't know where he's gittin' his strength from."

Henry ran forward and grasped his friend's arm. "Jim! Jim!" he pleaded. "Come with me."

Jim stared blankly as if he had no idea

"Take Yer Friend Out a' th' Road."

what Henry was saying. But he let himself be led off the road and onto the grass.

Moments later, the noisy clanging of large cannons coming toward them frightened Jim. He pulled away from Henry and began to run, stumbling, toward a clump of bushes.

Henry hurried after his friend. "No, Jim, wait! Where you goin'? Please wait, you'll hurt yourself!"

Jim stopped. "Leave me be, can't yeh?" he pleaded.

"Why, Jim, why? W-what's th' m-matter with you?" Henry gasped between sobs.

But Jim didn't answer. He just turned away and continued on. He seemed to be searching the ground for something... searching with an odd, blank stare in his eyes.

Finally, he stopped and stood motionless. He had reached the place he was searching for. His chest began to rise and fall with such violence, it was as if something was strangling him. Then his eyes rolled back into his

Jim Runs Away from Henry.

head until only white showed.

"Jim! Jim!" wailed Henry, falling to his knees at his friend's side.

"Leave me be! No! Don't tech me!" Jim whispered hoarsely. Then his body started convulsing. After several moments, it stiffened and fell forward, slow and straight, like a falling tree.

As he watched his friend's death movements, Henry's face twisted in agony. He sprang to his feet and gazed down.

Jim's unbuttoned jacket had fallen away from his body, and for the first time Henry saw his friend's wound. *His entire side had been shot away!*

"My Gawd!" Henry cried. "It looks like he's been chewed on by wolves!"

A fierce rage came over him, and he turned toward the battlefield, shaking his fist in frustration at the war that took the life of his childhood friend ... the war that gave Jim Conklin his red badge of courage!

His Entire Side Had Been Shot Away!

One Man Dead . . . One Near Death . . .

CHAPTER 9

Too Tired To Fight

Henry threw himself on the ground, grief-stricken and exhausted. When he finally looked up, he saw the tattered soldier staring down at Jim Conklin's corpse.

"He's gone now," the soldier said, "though I can't imagine where he got his strength from. An' I must say I ain't enjoyin' any great strength...m'self...these...days."

Hearing the soldier's voice weakening as he spoke, Henry looked up quickly. The man's feet were shaking and his face had turned blue. "Good Lord!" he cried. "You ain't goin' t' die too, are you?"

"Well, I'm feelin' pretty bad," said the tattered man, "but mebbe some pea soup an' a good bed'll fix me up. Besides, I can't die yet. I got me a wife an' a crowd a' young 'uns at home dependin' on me. . . . Say, did I tell yeh I got shot in m' head? An' when I put m' hand up t' m' head, them rebs shot me in th' arm. . . . Say, yeh look pretty peaked yerself. I bet yeh got a worser wound than yeh think yeh got, 'specially if'n it's inside mostly. Where's it at?"

Henry had been squirming uncomfortably as the tattered man spoke. Now he jumped up and glared at the man. He made a threatening motion with his hand as if to push him away. "Don't bother me!" he growled.

"Lord knows I don't want t' bother anybody," apologized the man.

Henry's couldn't stand any more talk and any more questions. He snarled, "Good-bye!" then turned to go.

"Don't Bother Me!"

"Where yeh goin', ol' buddy? Where yeh goin'?" cried the man. "See here, Ben Jamison, it ain't right fer an ol' friend like yeh t' go off with a bad hurt."

"I'm not Ben Jamison!" cried Henry. "You must be losin' your senses, man. I'm gettin' away from you!" He began running toward a fence at the end of the field.

"Come back, Ben. Yer my friend, Ben Jamison," pleaded the tattered man as he started wandering aimlessly in the field. "Come stay with me, please, Ben. I'm dyin', Ben."

Although the voice of the dying man was ringing in his ears, Henry continued running. "*He* knew... he knew my secret... he knew I ran away! I wish I were dead!" he sobbed. "I know I'll never be able t' keep the rest of the world from findin' out I'm a deserter. Soon, everyone'll know! Oh, I wish I was dead!"

Henry finally stopped running and sat down to rest at the top of a hill. He knew the

"Come Back, Ben."

battles were still raging from the roar of the artillery and the clouds of smoke in the distance. From where he was sitting, he saw a road filling up with retreating troops coming out of the woods and fields. Horses were pulling white-topped wagons, taking supplies to other battle locations.

Henry let out a sigh of relief. "Maybe I'm not alone after all," he reassured himself. "They're retreatin' from the battle too."

Soon, a fresh column of soldiers appeared on the road from the opposite direction. They were advancing into the battle.

As the two groups of soldiers came face to face, the officers leading the advancing column shouted to the retreating troops, "Make way! Let us pass!"

When their orders weren't immediately obeyed, the officers forced open a path by swinging the wooden handles of their rifles at the troops that blocked their way.

Seeing the straight, proud backs and eager

"Make Way! Let Us Pass!"

faces of the troops going to meet the enemy, Henry once again felt his spirits sink. "If only I could be like them," he whispered. "Maybe if I went back into battle and fought bravely and got killed, everyone would stand over my body and call me a hero! Then I'd have a red badge of courage."

Then, just as quickly, Henry's spirits lifted. "But then again, I could go back and *not* get killed. First, though, I'll have t' figure out a good story t' tell when I get back. Those fellers in my regiment'll be sure to ask where I've been and what I've been doin'. If I don't have answers or if I hesitate, they'll get suspicious. They'll sneer at me or make jokes. And they'd be sure t' watch me every second durin' the next battle t' see if I'm really a coward, t' see if I try t' run away. . . . No, I can't do it! I can't go back! I'm so hungry and so thirsty and so tired, I can't fight now."

"I Can't Fight Now."

Mobs Join Their Fleeing Comrades.

CHAPTER 10

A Red Badge?

Henry watched the advancing column until it was out of sight. Then he gaped at the mobs of men sweeping out of the woods and fields, joining their fleeing comrades on the road. "The battle must be gettin' pretty heavy if our boys are runnin' so fast to get away from it," he decided.

Behind the fleeing mob, smoke from the battle rose in clouds over the treetops. It was so thick, it nearly blocked out the stars that were just beginning to come out.

Cannons were booming, louder and louder, more and more often . . . but now the firing wasn't coming from the Union side at all. It was coming *only* from the Confederate side. When the mob realized this, they panicked!

"The fight is lost!" cried one soldier, horror-stricken. "Our army's defeated!"

"Keep runnin', man!" cried another. "Keep runnin' till yeh git away from this war!"

The news spread quickly through the mob, and the stampede was on. Big, burly men were leaping and scampering, their faces white with fear.

Henry hurried to join the fleeing troops. He had to know what was happening in the battle. He ran from one man to another, asking, "Where you comin' from? Why—"

But the fleeing soldiers seemed not to hear him or see him as they ran every which way. Artillery fire was now coming from all directions, and men were running toward it and away from it in total confusion, as they

"Where You Comin' From?"

shouted wildly to each other.

After rushing about and screaming at the retreating infantrymen, Henry finally seized one man by the arm. "What's happenin'? W-why are you runnin'? W-where—"

The soldier tried to pull away from Henry. "Let go a' me! Let go!" he screamed in fear and rage. His eyes were rolling in his head, and he was heaving and panting as he tried to catch his breath. The heavy rifle in his hand was slowing him down, but he seemed not to notice its weight.

Henry pulled frantically at the man's arm. "Wait! Please!" he pleaded.

"Let go a' me!"

"Please tell me why you're runnin'—*why?*"

"Here's why!" the man screamed furiously. He swung his rifle with all his force, and brought it crashing down on Henry's head.

A deafening thunder exploded inside him, and Henry released his hold on the man's arm. All the strength left his legs, and he

"Here's Why!"

sank to the ground, writhing in pain.

Once free of Henry's grip, the soldier fled down the road without a glance back.

Henry lay with his face in the dirt for several minutes before he opened his eyes. He tried to stand, but managed only to get to his knees. He took a few deep breaths to try to clear his head, but fell back on the grass again, groaning.

His body seemed to be fighting a battle with his mind. His body wanted him to lie and rest where he had fallen. But his mind feared that he would be trampled by men and horses and cannons if he were to lose consciousness on the grass. He fought the pain and stumbled to his feet.

Standing in the middle of the road, he reached his hand to the top of his head and nervously touched his wound. Gasping in pain, he took his hand away and found spots of blood on his fingers.

He was staring at the blood so intently he

A Painful Head Wound

didn't hear the bouncing cannon rolling toward him until the horses pulling it were almost on top of him. As he jumped out of the way and watched it pass, he saw masses of infantrymen, cavalrymen, and horse-drawn artillery following behind, heading for an opening in a long fence.

Moments later, the guns began to roar, and the orange lights of artillery fire lit up the evening sky all around him. Another battle had begun!

Henry stumbled along the narrow roadway littered with the remains of an earlier battle—guns, exploded parts of cannons, overturned wagons, and bodies of horses and men. Neither he nor any of the other fleeing soldiers paid any attention to these remains except to avoid stumbling and falling over them in the darkness.

The pain in his head seemed to be easing, but Henry was afraid to move too quickly for fear of opening up the wound again. He

Jumping Out of the Way

dragged his weary body along for hours, with his head hung forward and his shoulders drooping.

Some time around midnight, when the gunfire had quieted down a little, a cheerful voice beside him interrupted the silence. "Yeh seem t' be in a pretty bad way, m' boy. Are yeh?"

Henry didn't look up, but grunted.

The cheerful soldier ignored Henry's gruff reply and took him firmly under the arm. "I'm goin' yer way, m' boy," he said. "So's this whole gang. An' I guess I kin give yeh a lift. Yeh look like yeh sure kin use one."

As they walked along, the cheerful soldier asked question after question and ignored Henry's grunts and hesitant answers. "So yer with the 304th reg'ment? . . . Well, that means yer from N' York. . . . They in a fight t'day? . . . Guess that's where yeh got yer red badge, huh? . . . Say, I thought the 304th was way over in the center of the battle. . . . Oh, they

"I'm Goin' Yer Way, M' Boy."

was, huh? . . . It'll be a miracle if we find our reg'ments t'night. These woods is a reg'lar mess. It's so dark, yeh can't tell if yer fightin' with the Union or with the rebs."

He led Henry through a maze of woods filled with soldiers everywhere and managed to get them quickly past guards and patrols.

After several hours, he pulled Henry to a stop and pointed to a clearing. "There yeh are, m' boy! See that fire? That's where yer reg'ment is."

He took Henry's limp fingers in his warm strong hands, shaking the young man's hand, and then patted him on the shoulder. "Good-bye, m' boy and good luck t' yeh," he said. Then he turned and strode away, whistling happily.

Henry lifted his head for the first time. He suddenly realized in amazement, "Why, I never even saw what he looked like!"

"That's Where Yer Reg'ment Is."

"Halt! Halt! Who's There?"

CHAPTER 11

Returning to the 304th

Henry stumbled toward the campfire, fearful of what his regiment would say when they saw him. "They're sure to ridicule me," he decided. "But I've got no strength to make up a story. I'm just too tired and too hungry. And I hurt too much!"

Suddenly, a voice called out, "Halt! Halt! Who's there?" And the barrel of a rifle was pushed into his chest.

Henry recognized the voice. "That you, Tom Wilson?"

The rifle was lowered and a surprised voice

called out, "Henry? Henry Fleming? ... By ginger, I'm glad t' see yeh! I thought yeh was dead for sure."

Weakness was overcoming him quickly, and Henry knew he had to offer his story before any of his comrades started questioning him. "Yes, Tom," he began. "I've had an awful time. I got separated from the regiment an' I been way over on the right. Such terrible fightin' over there. Never seen any fightin' like it! I got shot, Tom. Shot in the head!"

Tom jumped to Henry's side. "What? Yeh got shot? Why didn't yeh say so first? Hold on a minute, Henry, and I'll get help. Corporal," he called, "over here!"

Within moments, Corporal Simpson joined them. "What yeh howlin' 'bout there, Wilson? ... Oh, Henry, hello. Why, I thought yeh was dead hours ago! We figgered we lost forty-two men, but they keep turnin' up ev'ry ten minutes or so. If it keeps up, reckon we'll git th' whole company back by mornin'. So, tell me,

"I Got Shot, Tom."

where was yeh, Henry?"

"Over on the right. I got separated," began Henry, feeling more comfortable now with his story.

But Tom interrupted quickly. "An' he got shot in th' head. We'd better see t' him right away." And putting his arm around Henry's shoulder, he added, "Gee, it must hurt like thunder!"

Henry leaned heavily on his friend. "Yes, it hurts," he said weakly, "hurts a heap!"

"I'll take care a' yeh," said Corporal Simpson, supporting Henry under the arms.

"Put Henry t' sleep in my blanket," said Tom, "an' here, take my canteen. It's full a' coffee. An' check his head over by th' fire. I get relieved in a couple a' minutes, and I'll be over t' take care a' him."

With his knees wobbling, Henry let the corporal lead him toward the fire. He sat down obediently and turned his head so the corporal could see the wound in the light.

Corporal Simpson Helps Henry.

Simpson whistled through his teeth when his fingers touched the dried blood. "Ah, here we are! Jest as I thought. Yeh've been grazed by a ball. It's raised a queer lump, jest as if some feller had slammed yeh on th' head with a club. It stopped bleedin', but yeh'll have one real big, hurtin' head in the mornin'."

Simpson handed Henry the canteen of coffee and went to arrange for Tom's relief. Henry seemed to forget that the canteen was in his hand as he stared into the crackling fire. Then he turned his gaze to the exhausted troops sleeping around it, some propped up against trees, others huddled in their blankets on the ground.

A few minutes later, Tom came running up, swinging a canteen of water on his arm. "Well now, Henry, we'll have yeh fixed up in jest a minute," he told his friend.

Tom bustled around, stirring up the fire so Henry would be warm and lifting the canteen

Examining a Queer Lump

to his friend's lips to make sure he drank all the coffee.

When Henry finished, he smiled at Tom. "That was sure good!" he said.

Tom took a large handkerchief from his pocket and folded it into a bandage. He soaked it with water from the canteen, then tied it around Henry's head, knotting it at the back of his neck.

After he stepped back to look over his work, he smiled and said, "There! Yeh look like th' devil, but I bet yeh feel better."

"Tom, my friend, this here cool cloth on my head feels as good as if it were my own mama's hand," Henry said gratefully.

"Why, thank yeh, Henry. Yer a brave un, though. Most men would a' been in th' hospital long ago with this kind a' red badge. A shot in th' head ain't no business t' fool with."

"Don't know how I can thank you, Tom."

"No need, Henry. Now let's put yeh t' bed

Tom Bandages Henry's Head.

and get yeh a good night's rest."

Tom helped Henry stand, then led him over to where the other soldiers were sleeping in groups. He picked up his own blankets and unrolled them. He spread the rubber blanket on the ground, then wrapped the woolen one around his friend's shoulders. "There now, lie down an' get some sleep."

Henry obeyed. "Thanks, Tom. This sure feels good. Why, this ground feels like the softest couch anyone could sleep on.... But wait! Where are you goin' to sleep?"

"Right down there next t' yeh, so I can watch over yeh."

"But I've got your—"

"Shet up an' go on t' sleep, Henry Fleming! Yer makin' a fool a' yerself!"

Henry stopped protesting. A pleasant drowsiness was spreading through him. He wrapped the warm blanket tighter around himself and let his head fall forward on his arm. In moments, his lids slowly closed over his eyes.

A Welcome Sleep for Henry

Seeing a Field of Corpses?

CHAPTER 12

Regaining His Strength

The next morning, Henry awoke before dawn. An icy dew covered his face, and he pulled the blanket over his nose and mouth. His still sleepy eyes stared out from under the blanket, and he saw the motionless bodies of the sleeping men all around him. "Am I surrounded by a field of corpses?" he gasped.

Then, in a moment, he came fully awake. "What kind of foolishness is fillin' my head? These are the same troops who were sleepin' here when I came last night. And that shootin' in the distance, I guess it didn't stop much since I fell asleep."

Henry turned his head toward the crackling fire. Tom was already there, making coffee for the men, while a few soldiers were chopping more wood.

Just then, bugles blew from near and far to wake the troops. The sleeping men grumbled and cursed as they stretched their stiff aching bodies and rubbed their eyes. Only the shouts from their officers got them moving with any speed.

Henry sat up and yawned. His hand carefully touched the bandage over his wound. His head felt as swollen as a melon.

Seeing his friend awake, Tom hurried over, asking, "Well, ol' man, how do yeh feel this mornin'?"

"My head's mighty sore, an' my stomach ain't feelin' much better," grumbled Henry.

"Let's see th' bandage," said Tom, moving the handkerchief. "Looks like it slipped."

"Gosh dern it!" exploded Henry. "You're the

Grumbling About His Sore Head

clumsiest man I ever saw! Are you wearin' mittens on your hands? Now go slow and easy. You ain't nailin' down some carpet! You're bandagin' a gunshot wound."

Tom answered his friend's angry outburst with calm, soothing words. "Well, well, sounds like yeh need t' get some food in yer belly. Then mebbe yeh'll feel better."

They went over to the fire, where Tom roasted some fresh meat on a stick for Henry. Then he filled a little black tin cup of hot coffee and sat back to watch Henry devour the food. Tom smiled broadly.

Once the meal had filled his stomach, Henry sat back and studied Tom with great seriousness. "Tom, you've changed mightily these last few days. Once, you'd have been right angry at the way I spoke to you. Once, all you cared about was yourself. Now, your thoughts are for all the men around you."

"I guess I was a pretty big fool then," Tom said quietly, "even though it was only days

Tom Feeds His Friend.

ago...Say, Henry, what yeh think our chances are? All th' officers say we've got th' rebs in a pretty tight box."

"I don't know about that," replied Henry. "What I seen over on the right makes me think it's the other way around. From where I was yesterday, it looked as if we was gettin' a good poundin'."

"I thought we was *givin'* the poundin'."

"Not a bit! If that's what you thought, man, you didn't see nothin' of the fight and—oh, Lord, I forgot to tell you, Jim Conklin's dead. Shot in the side."

"Oh, Jim! Poor feller! Our regiment lost over half th' men yesterday. I thought they was all dead, but they kept a-comin' back last night. They'd been scattered all over, wanderin' around th' woods, fightin' with other regiments. Jest like yeh, Henry."

"So what?" demanded Henry. He was suddenly afraid that Tom was about to question him about where he was yesterday.

"Jim Conklin's Dead."

"So, I guess we's jest lucky we came out alive." Then Tom began fidgeting nervously with the buttons on his jacket. "Uh—uh—uh, Henry," he stammered.

"What is it, man?" snapped Henry. "Spit it out."

"W-well," mumbled Tom. He gulped and his face turned bright red with embarrassment. "I guess yeh might as well give me back them letters. Yeh don't need t' send 'em t' my family now."

Henry had to keep from grinning at his friend's discomfort. He slowly reached his hand inside his jacket and took out the thick yellow envelope, all the while watching Tom squirm.

Tom couldn't know that Henry was thinking, "I could've used these letters as a weapon to silence Tom if he became suspicious of my story. But now I can be generous and return them to him. After all, no one questioned me, no one discovered anythin'. Everythin' I did, I

Returning Tom's Envelope

did in the darkness, so no one saw my cowardly retreat. I'm still a man!"

Tom seemed to be suffering his embarrassment silently as he shifted his weight from foot to foot and stared at the ground. He was ashamed of having feared death and giving Henry his letters.

Henry was now smiling smugly. He felt very generous, very proud of himself, as he pictured glowing scenes in his mind. "I can see it now. When I return home after this war and tell everyone excitin' stories of these mighty battles, how impressed they'll be! How proud they'll be of my bravery!"

The order to fall into formation snapped Henry out of his daydreams. Tom brought him a rifle and fresh supplies, and together the two men stood at attention waiting for the command to march.

Picturing His Return Home

Resting in the Trenches

CHAPTER 13

From Coward to Hero!

The 304th Regiment was marched to a line of damp trenches along the edge of some woods. They relieved a regiment that had been holding that line for several weeks.

The low embankments piled in front of the trenches gave protection to the troops, even allowing some of them to lean up against these hills of dirt and go to sleep.

In front of the embankments lay an open field, with only cut stumps of trees rising out of the foggy ground. From beyond the field came the occasional sputtering of rebel skirmishers firing into the fog.

Henry leaned his chest against the embankment and peered up and down the line and across at the woods. The sound of gunfire from battles going on around him and the roaring of cannons on both sides made it impossible for him to even talk to any of his comrades. As they waited, the men could only listen to the firing and guess at what was happening.

Most of them believed their troops were being defeated, and when there was a lull in the firing and the men could talk, they blamed their officers for the defeat.

The waiting continued until the sun's rays were beginning to shine down through the trees. Then the regiment was ordered out of the trenches and on a retreating march back through the woods. Behind them, they could hear the triumphant cheers and yells of the enemy.

These yells enraged Henry. "By jiminy,

Henry Peers Across at the Woods.

we're bein' commanded by a lunkhead of a general!" he exploded.

Many of the soldiers around him agreed.

Tom heaved a weary sigh. "Mebbe it wasn't all his fault. He did th' best he knowed. We jest had the bad luck t' get licked often."

"Don't we fight like the devil? Don't we do all that men can?" shouted Henry.

Then he stopped. Had those words actually come from his lips? For a moment, he looked around him, feeling guilty. But then he realized that no one doubted his courage . . . no one doubted his right to say those words or have those feelings. So he went on.

"I don't see any sense in fightin' an' fightin', an' always losin' because a' some derned old lunkhead of a general!"

One sarcastic man nearby snapped, "Mebbe yeh think yeh fought th' whole battle by yerself yesterday, Fleming."

Those words sent shivers of fear through Henry. Did the man know his secret? "W-why

Arguing About Their Officers

no," he stammered, "I don't think I fought the whole battle by myself at all."

Still, Henry felt threatened. "I'd best keep quiet durin' the rest of the march," he thought. "I don't need to call attention to myself."

As the march through the forest continued, the troops became more and more sullen. They muttered more and cursed more each time they heard firing begin in the distance.

When the 304th was halted in a clearing, they were soon joined by other regiments and ordered to set up their battle lines again. So the men dug trenches, or lay down behind embankments, branches, tree trunks, or whatever other protection they had collected.

As the men faced the shouts of the enemy infantry, their own cannons were set up in position behind them. No shots were fired yet, and everyone waited breathlessly.

"Good Gawd!" grumbled Henry. "We're bein' chased around like rats! Nobody seems to

Other Regiments Join the 304th.

know where we go or why we go. We just get sent from one place to another, and get beaten here and there, and what for? Why were we marched here? So the rebs could take pot shots at us? There ain't no reason for it. It's that derned old—"

Tom interrupted his friend, trying to calm him. "It'll turn out all right in th' end, Henry. Jest yeh wait an' see."

"You always talk like a preacher, Tom Wilson! You an' your confidence! Don't—"

The lieutenant had been pacing behind them when he heard the arguing. He had to put a stop to it even though he was feeling the same frustrations as his men. "You boys shut right up!" he ordered. "There's no need wastin' your breath jawin' like a lot a' old hens. All you got to do is fight, and you'll get plenty a' that in about ten minutes. I figger the rebs'll attack as soon as the sun's up. Less talkin' and more fightin' is what's best for you boys!"

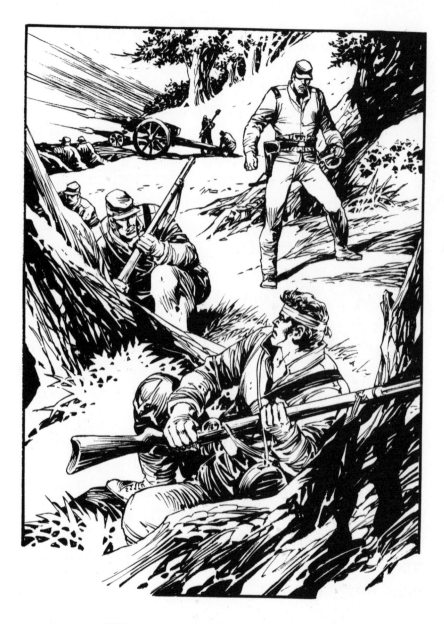

"You Boys Shut Right Up!"

THE RED BADGE OF COURAGE

The men were too afraid to reply, and the lieutenant resumed his pacing, tugging nervously at his mustache as he strode to and fro in the morning silence.

When the sun was directly overhead, a single rifle shot flashed into the woods at the regiment. A moment later, it was followed by many others. Explosions from the enemy's cannons mixed with the cracklings of their rifles. The big battle had begun!

The men of the 304th waited for the enemy to approach. Wide-eyed, worn, and exhausted, they stood as if they were tied to the stake, taking their last breath before they were executed!

As he crouched behind a tree, Henry nervously twisted his fingers on his rifle. His pulse began to pound and his eyes burned with hate. The bandage around his head had a new spot of blood on it. It was as if his rage against the enemy and against his own officers was pounding so heavily inside his head

Eyes Burning with Hatred!

that it opened his wound again.

Henry muttered to Tom, "Oh, how I wish I could use my rifle t' smash in the victory smiles those rebs are probably smilin' now!"

When the order came for the regiment to begin firing, Henry was the first and fastest to begin. He kept stuffing cartridges into his rifle and pounding them in with his clanking ramrod. Grunting fiercely, he ran out from behind the tree, rushed forward, and pulled the trigger.

He kept repeating his actions over and over again until his rifle barrel grew so hot that ordinarily he wouldn't have been able to touch it. But now his palms felt no pain. His fingers and hands knew only the actions they had to take. Even when the enemy seemed to be retreating and there was a lull in the shelling, Henry's rifle—*and only Henry's*—continued firing.

During that lull, a hoarse laugh reached Henry's ears and a voice brought him to his

The First and Fastest To Fire

senses. "Yeh derned infernal fool! Don't yeh know enough t' quit when there ain't nothin' t' shoot at?"

Henry froze. With his rifle raised to shooting position, he looked down the line. His comrades were all staring at him in astonishment. He turned his bewildered eyes to the front again and saw the smoke lifting. The battlefield was deserted!

"Oh," he said, slowly lowering his rifle and finally understanding what had happened.

He returned to his comrades and threw himself down on the grass. His skin was burning hot, and the battle noises were still ringing in his ears. He groped for his canteen and took a long drink.

The lieutenant came over to where Henry was sprawled out on the grass and called out loud enough for the regiment to hear, "By heavens, Fleming, if I had ten thousand wild men like you, I could end this war in less than a week!"

The Battlefield Is Deserted!

THE RED BADGE OF COURAGE

During the battle, his comrades had been watching with astonishment as Henry loaded and fired, loaded and fired, long after they, themselves, had stopped. Now, their smudged, blackened faces could not hide the wonder and respect they felt as they stared at him.

"By thunder, I bet this army'll never see another regiment like ours or another war devil like Henry Fleming!" shouted one man.

"Lost a pile a' men, them rebels did," added another, "thanks t' us an' t' Henry!"

"And in an hour, they're goin' t' lose a pile more," boasted a third confidently.

Henry was smiling as he listened to his comrades. He, too, was proud. "I went into this battle believin' I was a coward, and I came out of it a hero!"

Admiration from His Comrades

"I Think I Saw a Stream."

CHAPTER 14

The Mule Drivers

It was during this pause in the fighting that Henry heard screams of pain. He and Tom rushed to a wounded soldier who was writhing in agony on the grass nearby.

"Maybe some water will help his pain," suggested Henry.

"I think I saw a stream off t' th' left as we marched here," said Tom.

"Then let's go get some before the shootin' starts up again."

With the lieutenant's permission, Tom and Henry gathered the canteens of the thirsty troops around them and headed off through the woods.

Up one path and down another they searched for the stream, but with no luck. Once away from the smoke of their own line, they stood on a hill and got a full view of the fighting. The Union infantry was marching to the rear, retreating from the Confederate army.

When Henry and Tom finally gave up their search for water, they started to retrace their steps back to the regiment. As they came to a small clearing, they saw the commanding general of their division and his aide reining their horses to a halt. Their own regimental captain was riding toward the general from the opposite direction.

Henry and Tom halted their steps, though they made sure to stay hidden in the bushes.

"Let's listen," whispered Henry. "Maybe we'll learn what's happenin' out there."

"Mebbe it's real important," added Tom.

As the captain came alongside, the general

Hoping To Learn What's Happening

announced, "The enemy's forming for another charge." And he pointed off to his right.

"Where do you figure they'll attack, sir?" asked the captain.

"My guess is it'll be directed against General Whiterside's division. And I fear the rebs'll break through their line unless we get him more troops to help stop them."

"I don't see how we can stop them, sir."

"I don't either, unless... what troops can you spare from the regiments under your command, Captain?"

The captain thought for a moment, "Well, sir, I had to order in the 12th to help the 76th, so I haven't really got any to spare... unless you want to consider the 304th. Only problem there, sir, is they're kind of wild and rather stupid. They fight like a bunch of mule drivers. Still, they're the only spare regiment."

Henry and Tom looked at each other, first in astonishment, then in rage at what they

"They Fight Like a Bunch of Mule Drivers."

had just heard their captain call them.

"We fight with our hearts an' souls, and he has the nerve to call us mule drivers!" Henry snarled under his breath to Tom.

The general ordered the captain, "Then get the 304th ready! I'll watch the developments from here and send you word when to attack. It'll probably be in about five minutes."

The captain saluted and swung his horse around. Behind him, the general called out grimly, "I don't think many of your mule drivers will come out of this battle alive.

Henry and Tom turned to each other once more, this time exchanging looks of fear. Then they quickly and quietly made their way back to their line.

As he led the way through the woods, a sudden realization hit Henry, and he shared his feelings with Tom. "Do you realize our whole regiment's not all that important in this war, at least not to the general? He hardly needs us. We're nothin' more than a broom he's usin'

A Grim Prediction

to sweep out the forest . . . but I suppose that's the way war is."

"Fleming! Wilson!" The lieutenant's voice interrupted Henry. "How long does it take you to get water? Where've you been?"

The excited faces on the two soldiers quickly silenced the lieutenant.

"We're goin t' be the ones to charge!" cried Tom. "We're goin' t' be the ones to attack! Us! Our regiment!"

"Charge?" said the lieutenant with a broad smile. "Well, now finally this is goin' to be real fightin'!"

A group of soldiers surrounded Henry and Tom, full of questions and doubts.

"Are we? Sure 'nough?"

"Well, I'll be derned!"

"Charge? What fer?"

"Yer lyin', Wilson!"

"I swear!" argued Tom. "Sure as shootin'."

"He ain't lyin'," Henry defended his friend. "We heard the general talkin'."

Excited Over Their News!

THE RED BADGE OF COURAGE

Minutes later, the regiment's officers began scurrying back and forth, forming the men into a tighter line. As they took their positions, the men seemed to be bravely and seriously concentrating on the battle that was about to begin.

Henry and Tom exchanged long, knowing looks. Each man remembered the general's words... words they had *not* repeated to their comrades... words that they had kept secret ... *"I don't think many of your mule drivers will come out of this battle alive!"*

When a shaggy man near them groaned that they'd "all git swallowed up by them rebs," Henry knew it was true. Still, he didn't hesitate or move from his position.

He nodded silently to Tom, and his friend nodded in return. Both men were now ready to accept the dangers of the battle ahead. Both knew that many of their men—perhaps even they themselves—would surely be killed!

Remembering the General's Words

The Signal To Attack

CHAPTER 15

Protecting the Flag

The captain galloped up and down the line, waving his hat—the signal to begin the attack. With slow, cautious steps, the men left the safety of the woods and broke into a wild run when they reached the clearing.

Yellow flames from enemy artillery came at them from all directions. The line to the right and left of Henry seemed to split from the center, then form into small, separate groups. The men were running wildly and cheering madly. They were convinced that no enemy could stop them, no matter how great the odds were against them.

Henry ran desperately toward a distant clump of trees. "That must be where the rebs are hidin'," he told himself as his breath came in gasps.

His face was growing redder from his desperate run and almost matched the blood spot on the rag tied around his head. His lips were drawn hard and tight, and his eyes were shining with a wild glare. That, combined with his disordered, dirty clothes and his wildly swinging rifle, gave Henry Fleming the look of an insane soldier.

Though his gaze was fixed straight ahead, out of the corner of his eye Henry saw a shell tumble and explode furiously into the middle of a group of men. The soldiers threw up their hands to shield their eyes as the explosion flung them in every direction.

Other soldiers, hit by bullets, fell in agony. They formed a trail of wounded bodies and motionless corpses left behind by the regiment

An Exploding Shell

as it advanced.

Still, Henry kept running blindly into the smoke and gunfire. He wasn't aware that he was in the lead. And after a while, he wasn't even aware that his comrades were beginning to tire.

Instead of running headlong into the hot smoke, the men hesitated. They waited for the smoke to clear and show them the battle-field. With their strength weakened, with their lungs gasping for air, they were no longer the wild, attacking machines they were earlier; they were cautious, fearful men once more.

This caution and fear stopped them in the middle of the battlefield even though the enemy continued firing. Men looked around and saw their comrades dropping to the ground, moaning and shrieking. This sight seemed to paralyze them. Dazed and almost in a stupor, they let their rifles drop limply to their sides as their eyes moved slowly from

The Troops Are Paralyzed.

body to body.

Not even the roar of the lieutenant could rouse them from their stupor as he yelled, "Come on, you fools! Come on! You can't stay here in the middle of the field."

But the men stood frozen, staring blankly at him. Tom Wilson was the first to recover from the daze. He dropped to his knees and fired off a shot into the woods. The shot finally shook the men out of their stupor, and they raised their rifles and began firing once again.

Driven across the open field by their officers, the regiment began moving forward. They stopped only to fire and reload every few steps.

They entered a small grove and moved from tree to tree cautiously. Enemy fire was still coming at them from across a large open field at the end of the grove. The thick smoke made it impossible to see farther than the tips of their rifles. Still, the lieutenant was urging

"You Can't Stay Here."

them forward.

"Come on, lunkheads! We'll all be killed if we stay here. We've only got to go across that field," he roared, pointing to a large open space between them and the enemy line.

None of the men seemed ready to follow the lieutenant, except Henry and Tom. They hurried to him, and the three men ran down the line, shouting to their comrades, "Come on! Come on!"

The sergeant carrying the Union colors scrambled out in front of the line. A moment later, the shabby-looking troops of the 304th seemed to get inspiration from the sight of their flag, and they surged forward. Rifle shots and yellow bursts of flame came at them from the woods.

Henry lowered his head and ran like a madman to reach the safety of the woods before a bullet could hit him. With his eyes almost closed, his mind formed a picture of his country's flag. "What a beautiful thing it is!" he

Inspired by Their Flag

thought. "I must never let it be conquered or destroyed! I must keep it from harm and it will keep me from harm too!"

At that moment, the sergeant carrying the flag gave a loud cry as a bullet tore into his chest. His body froze and his eyes flew open in disbelief. But his stiff arms kept the flag held high.

Henry sprang for the flag, clutching at the pole with his free hand. At the same moment, Tom lunged for it as well. The two men tried to jerk it out of the dead man's hands, but even in death the sergeant refused to loosen his grip. He was determined to carry his country's colors into battle.

Henry and Tom wrenched furiously and finally freed the flag from the dead man. His raised arms, stiff from keeping the flag held high, swung down onto Tom's shoulder as if to protest the theft of the colors. Helpless now, the dead man swayed backward and crumbled to the ground.

Wrenching the Flag from a Dead Man

Henry Gets the Flag.

CHAPTER 16

The Mule Drivers' Revenge!

"Give it t' me! Let go of it!" shouted Henry as he pulled on the pole.

"No, let me keep it!" cried Tom.

For each of these young soldiers, carrying the flag into battle showed a willingness to risk his life by not carrying a gun. It took courage for a soldier to lay down his rifle and be defenseless, and both Henry and Tom were now showing that kind of courage.

With a hard, determined pull, Henry managed to get the flag away from Tom. Then he had a moment to look around at the rest of the regiment. He was horrified to see the troops slowly backing away from the battle, into the safety of the woods behind them.

"Where you goin'?" Henry howled. "Stay here an' fight! Shoot into them!"

"What's the good a' shootin' at walls?" cried one soldier.

"They got us beat!" wailed another.

"It's them lunkhead officers!" shouted still another.

But when the lieutenant ordered the rest of the men back into the woods to regroup, Henry and Tom headed back to join them.

Frustrated and angry, Henry mumbled to Tom, "The way our troops retreated proved those officers were right when they called us mule drivers. If only we'd taken some enemy ground and advanced, we would've had our revenge against that lunkhead general!"

Henry looked out at the enemy with hatred and rage, but he felt greater hatred and rage for the cold-hearted general and harsh captain

"Stay Here an' Fight!"

who labeled him and his comrades mule drivers without even knowing them!

Still, he held the flag high and joined the lieutenant as he regrouped the regiment. Together, they began pushing and pulling the men into the battle. Those who had the courage to join the line and advance faced round after round of merciless gunfire. Those who still had some courage left after that gunfire were shaken when they saw their comrades falling beside them or running away from the fighting.

The heavy clouds of smoke from the gunfire made it almost impossible to see the enemy. But a sudden break in the smoke revealed the battlefield.

Peering through the break, Henry gasped, "By Gawd! They're about to attack again! There's thousands of 'em!"

With rasping yells, the rebels opened fire. Hundreds of flames spurted out toward the retreating regiment, and clouds of smoke once

Pushing and Pulling the Men into Battle

more separated the two armies.

The Union soldiers panicked. Screaming wildly, they began running in all directions, trying to escape the bullets that were smashing into them.

"I could a' swore that the regiment over there was one a' ours," cried one soldier, pointing to the right where the gunfire pouring down on them was coming from.

"Mebbe it is," yelled another, running alongside him. "Mebbe they're lost and don't know they're shootin' at us!"

These words were passed from man to man, sending a wave of hysteria throughout the regiment. A private who had been calm and courageous during the battle now stopped running and sank to the ground. Burying his face in his hands, he wept, "We're doomed!" A corporal who had defended the actions of his officers all along now shrieked, "The general's gone mad! He deserves t' die!"

Henry walked calmly into the midst of this

"We're Doomed!"

hysterical mob and raised the flag higher, for all the men to see. Though his hands were trembling and he was having trouble catching his breath, he stood firmly, hoping that the sight of their country's colors would give the men the courage to continue the battle.

Tom came up to him and solemnly said, "Well, Henry, I guess this is good-bye."

"Oh, shut up, you fool!" cried Henry, turning away from his friend to watch the officers trying to get the men into position to fight off the attack.

"Here they come!" cried the lieutenant. "They're right on top of us! Shoot!" And the rest of his words were lost as thundering gunfire burst out from the regiment.

Henry stared at the approaching enemy. They were so close now, he could see their faces and every detail of their light-gray uniforms. He called out to Tom who was still beside him, "Looks like they were advancin'

"I Guess This Is Good-bye."

on us through the smoke and didn't rightly know how close they were till the lieutenant spotted them and we opened fire."

The two armies were exchanging gunfire at such a rapid pace that the smoke never had a chance to clear. All Henry could see were flashes of flame and dark clouds of smoke. All he could hear were angry gunshots and clanging ramrods. All he could do was continue to hold the flag high as his comrades went on firing.

Soon, the bullets from the rebels slowed down. "Hold your fire!" the lieutenant called to the regiment.

The men stood still, gazing as the smoke cleared. The battlefield soon came into view. Not a living Confederate soldier was to be seen . . . only an empty ground with scattered corpses twisted into grotesque shapes.

The Union soldiers sprang out from behind their trees and bushes. They began shouting and dancing for joy.

An Empty Battlefield!

"They're gone!"

"We chased 'em, fer sure!"

"An' them officers said we couldn't do it."

"Guess we showed 'em!"

"Guess we earned our red badges!"

Henry thrust the flag pole into the ground in front of him and saluted proudly. "You *did* keep us from harm," he said with solemn dignity.

Then, smiling at the troops of the 304th Regiment, he added, "It looks like the mule drivers have had their revenge!"

"The Mule Drivers Have Had Their Revenge!"

Veterans Tease the Young Troops.

CHAPTER 17

Criticism and Praise

With the fighting over, the weary, battered troops of the 304th hurried back to their own lines. On the way, they passed a group of haggard veterans from another company. The men lay resting in the shade of some trees. Seeing the young troops, the veterans began to tease them.

"What yeh comin' back fer?"

"Where yeh been?"

"Was it too hot fer yeh out there, sonny?"

"Goin' home t' mama now?"

The weary regiment tried to ignore these

teasing insults. But the cruel words made several of the men feel like criminals for having retreated, even though they won the battle. And they hung their heads in shame as they trudged along...all except Henry, who glared at the veterans.

Once back at their own lines, Henry and Tom turned to look at the battlefield they had just won.

"By Gawd!" exclaimed Henry. "I figured we took a whole lot more ground than this!"

"An' those woods where we had that last skirmish are much nearer than I would a' guessed too," added Tom.

The fighting time also lasted much shorter than Henry thought. "I guess my mind's just playin' tricks on me," he decided. "There's just no takin' the measure of a battle when you're in the middle of it!"

As the troops flung themselves down and began gulping water from their canteens, the general who had called them mule drivers

A Drink After the Battle

came galloping along the line. He had lost his hat and his hair streamed wildly about his angry face. He jerked furiously at the reins on his horse as he pulled to a halt in front of the colonel.

"By thunder, MacChesnay, what an awful mess you made of this battle!" he roared. "Why in heaven's name did you stop your men a hundred feet this side of success? Just a hundred feet more and you would have made a great charge. But as it is, all your men seem to be able to do is dig trenches in the mud! You've got a command of mud diggers!"

The men were listening intently, hoping the colonel would come to their defense, to explain that the regiment was *not* made up of mud diggers, but courageous fighting men.

Instead, the colonel simply shrugged and calmly explained, "Oh, well, sir, we went as far as we could."

"As far as you could! Well, that wasn't very

"Just a Hundred Feet More..."

far! Your orders were to divert the enemy troops *away* from General Whiterside. But just listen to that firing in the woods. *That's* how well you succeeded. Whiterside's being attacked now!" With that, the general wheeled his horse around and rode away.

The lieutenant approached the colonel. "Sir," he said firmly, "I don't care what that man is—a general or what—but if he says our boys didn't put up a good fight out there, well, he's a damned fool!"

"Lieutenant," began the colonel severely, "this is my problem and—"

The lieutenant backed away. "All right, sir, all right." But he was proud that he had spoken out in defense of his regiment.

As the news of the criticism of the regiment went down the line, the men were bewildered. It had to be a mistake! . . . But then they realized that their efforts were unimportant, and this angered every man in the regiment.

"He's a Damned Fool!"

"What does he want from us?" raged Tom. "We weren't out there pitchin' horseshoes!"

Henry seemed calm enough as he explained, "The general probably didn't see anythin' of the battle at all and just got mad because we didn't do exactly what he wanted. But we know we did our best and fought good. It's just our awful luck!"

"Well, there's no fun in fightin' for people when everythin' yeh do—no matter what—don't please 'em," shouted Tom. "Mebbe next time, I'll stay behind an' let 'em go to th' devil with their charge!"

"Next time, let that lunkhead general come onto the battlefield with us. We'll show him what—" But Henry didn't get a chance to finish, for several men came running up, their faces eager to share some news.

"Oh, Fleming!" cried one man as he and the others circled around Henry and Tom. "Yeh got t' hear this. The colonel met yer lieutenant right near us, and he asked him who was the

Eager To Share Their News

lad who carried the flag. When the lieutenant said it was Fleming, the colonel said 'He's a good man.' And the lieutenant he went on t' say, 'And so's the feller Wilson who was at the head a' the charge with Fleming, both a' them howlin' like Indians.' And the colonel then sez—now listen to this—the colonel sez, *'They deserve t' be major generals!'*"

"Major generals? No!" exclaimed Tom in disbelief. "Yer lyin'!"

"Go to blazes!" added Henry. "He never said that. You're makin' it up."

But Henry and Tom knew it was true. Their faces turned red in embarrassment, and although they protested, they were actually thrilled. As the two friends exchanged secret glances, congratulating each other, their anger at the general and captain was quickly forgotten. All they felt was affection and gratitude for their colonel and their lieutenant.

"Now Listen to This. . . ."

Joining the Fighting Again

CHAPTER 18

The Final Battle

A short while later, a Confederate attack started up against two other regiments on a nearby hill. From where he was standing, with the flag clutched in his hands, Henry was able to watch the fierce fighting and hear the yells and shouts from both sides.

Soon the battle came closer, and the 304th Regiment joined the fighting. With wild cries of rage, the men eagerly pounded cartridges into their rifle barrels with clanging ramrods and furiously returned the gunfire. Before long, the dark, heavy smoke was clinging to their blackened faces, with only their glowing eyes and white teeth showing.

The rebels were coming closer, so close that Henry could see their weary, excited faces. As the regiment started firing at them, the rebs ducked behind the protection of a long stone fence. From the safety of this position, they began to fire direct hits on the Union soldiers, cheering and shouting insults at their easy targets.

The Northern regiments, however, did not return the shouts or insults of the rebels.

"We've got to hold this ground!" cried the lieutenant.

"Yea, we got t' show that general we're no mud diggers," grumbled a soldier bitterly.

Even with all the shooting going on around him, Henry didn't regret he was holding a flag instead of a rifle. His pride in his comrades was growing with each shot they fired. And his hatred for the general and captain was growing with each shot too. "If it takes

The Rebels Fire Direct Hits.

my dead body, lyin' torn and bloody, on the battlefield to make those officers regret callin' us mule drivers and mud diggers, then I'll gladly give my life. It would be my final revenge on them!"

As the fighting continued, Henry saw his comrades dropping everywhere. Some crawled for places to hide; others were silent corpses. A sergeant was shot through the cheek, and blood was pouring out of the gaping hole that had been his mouth.

The lieutenant was hit in the right arm, but continued directing his troops' movements with his left. With so many casualties and so many weak, exhausted men, however, there wasn't much of a regiment to direct. Still, the troops held their ground, just as they had been ordered to.

Then the voice of the colonel called out from the back of the line. "Charge!" he shouted. "We must attack! Attack!"

Henry looked out across the field to the

Directing His Troops' Movements

enemy's position. He nodded silently, then turned to Tom. "The colonel's right. We have to attack. If we stay here or retreat, we'll all be killed. But if we attack, there's a chance that we can push those rebels away from the fence."

"I don't know if th' men'll follow those orders an' attack," said Tom, frowning. "They've already been pushed 'bout as far as any men could be."

But to Tom's surprise, the men were nodding at the colonel's orders. And at the command to charge, they quickly fastened their bayonets onto their rifle barrels and sprang forward with eager shouts.

The troops seemed to completely forget their weak, tired bodies as they rushed feverishly toward the fence. They seemed filled with new strength as they came face to face with the blasts of their enemies' rifles.

At the front of the charge, Henry held the colors high with his right arm while waving

Rushing Feverishly Toward the Enemy!

his left in circles to urge on the men behind him. The soldiers were hurling themselves into battle with a reckless enthusiasm.

"Gawd, they'll wind up a pile of corpses, the way they're goin' in such a frenzy," thought Henry. "They're not even thinkin'."

As he ran faster and faster, with the cheering regiment beside and behind him, Henry felt himself catching this battle madness. "Let's show 'em!" he shouted. "Let's crash into those rebs with a crushin' blow!"

But that crushing blow was not to be struck. For as the smoke rolled off, it revealed rebel soldiers running *away* from the battle. As they ran, some turned to fire their last bullets into the attacking Union soldiers.

Only one part of the rebel line was holding firm. With their tattered flag flying above them, a stubborn group of Confederate soldiers continued firing from behind the stone fence and yelling at the attacking Union troops.

Firing Their Last Bullets

THE RED BADGE OF COURAGE

As the regiment closed the distance between themselves and this small group, Henry's gaze was fixed on the badly torn Confederate flag. "What bloody battles it must have flown over!" he whispered. "How proud I'd be to capture it!"

As he reached the fence where the rebels were holding out, Henry lunged for their flag. His own flying colors tilted toward the enemy's. The bird-shaped brass tips on each pole pointed at each other like two eagles getting their claws and beaks ready to attack.

As the rest of the troops followed Henry to the fence, they roared a blast of fire at the fleeing enemy. Some of the rebels were still firing back, but nothing could stop the Union soldiers now. Yelling and shrieking, they leaped onto the fence and over it.

Henry and Tom jumped into the group of rebels. Some of the men were stretched out on the ground; others were writhing on their

Two Eagles Ready To Attack

knees. The flag bearer was struggling to stand upright in spite of the bullet holes that had just riddled his body. His face was twisted in pain and desperation as he hugged his flag to him. Then he stumbled and staggered, trying to carry it to safety.

Tom sprang at the flag and wrenched it free. "I've got it!" he cried at the same moment that the flag bearer gasped and stiffened, then fell to the ground, dead.

The elated Union troops cheered wildly as Tom waved his captured prize. Those men who still wore hats or caps flung them high into the air.

A little farther down the line, other troops had swooped down on a pocket of four rebel soldiers. The prisoners now sat at the feet of their captors.

One veteran rebel soldier was gripping his wounded leg and glaring up at the Union men. He began swearing and cursing at his captors.

"I've Got It!"

Another, much younger, soldier was smiling and chatting with the Union troops about the battles they had both fought in.

The third prisoner sat in stony silence. When the soldiers tried to question him, his only reply was "Go t' blazes!"

The fourth man refused to raise his eyes. He seemed ashamed to have been captured and couldn't face his comrades or his captors.

Henry and Tom, meanwhile, had walked off by themselves, away from the victory celebrations, and sat in some tall grass.

Planting his flag in the ground in front of him, Henry reached out to shake Tom's hand. "Congratulations, Private Wilson!"

Tom planted his flag beside Henry's and smiled at his friend. "An' congratulations t' yeh too, Private Fleming! We sure done a good job t'day!"

Rebel Prisoners

No Time to Sit and Rest

CHAPTER 19

From Boy to Man

Though there were some occasional bursts of artillery in the distance, the crashes of musketry that had surrounded the troops for days had completely stopped. Soldiers were marching away in all directions. Their cannons trailed leisurely after them.

Soon, the 304th Regiment was ordered to fall into line. Henry and Tom rejoined their comrades, who were stretching and grunting as they stood up.

"Can't they even give us some time t' rest?" grumbled one man.

"What now?" asked another.

The men trudged slowly back across the same field they had charged across only a while ago. They entered the same woods they had been in earlier and joined up with other dust-covered regiments to form their division once again.

When they reached the river they had waded across only the day before, Henry turned and looked back over the trampled ground they had just left. Scorched artillery shells and exploded cannons were strewn all over it.

"Well, I guess this one's over... at least for now," Henry said with a sigh.

Tom looked back too. "I sure am glad!"

As Henry thought back over the last two days, he had mixed feelings about his performance. He was proud of his courage in carrying the flag as he led the regiment. But the memory of his desertion during the first battle made him blush with shame. He felt even more ashamed when he remembered how he

A Last Look at the Trampled Ground

had repaid the tattered soldier's concern for his wound by leaving him to die alone in the field. Henry quickly looked at his comrades. Could they see his shame?

"Is somethin' wrong, Henry?" asked Tom, noticing his friend's discomfort.

Henry shook his head and kept his eyes straight ahead as he marched along.

A heavy rain began to fall. As it washed the dirt and smoke from his face, Henry felt it wash the guilty thoughts from his mind as well. "I was a coward when I first went into battle," he told himself. "I was just a boy and didn't know any better. But in the last two days, I saw death all around and faced it many times myself. In those two days, I grew up and earned my red badge of courage!"

When the late afternoon sun came out, it shone down on fresh meadows and cool brooks, on a world that hoped one day for peace, and on a boy who was ready to face the next battle as a man!

Ready for the Next Battle as a Man!

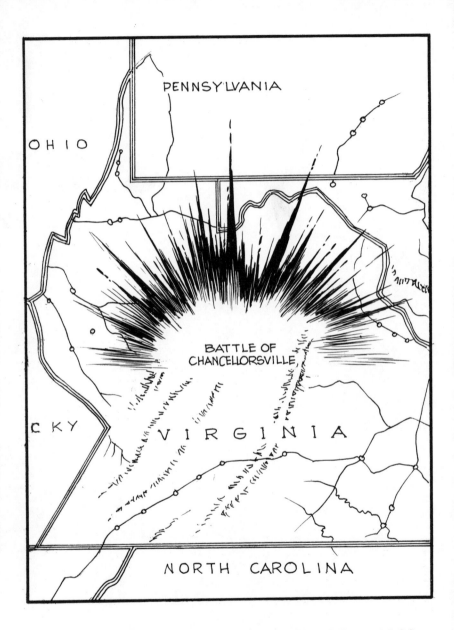

The Battle of Chancellorsville: May, 1863